JOE'S WEIRD WORLD

Kanako & Yuzuru

Slimed! 3

Wolfed! 18

Published by Pearson Education Limited, Edinburgh Gate, Harlow, Essex, CM20 2JE.

www.pearsonschools.co.uk

Text © Frank Rodgers 2013

Designed by Georgia Styring
Original illustrations © Kanako & Yuzuru 2013
Illustrated by Kanako & Yuzuru, Good Illustration Ltd
Cover design by Kanako & Yuzuru

The right of Frank Rodgers to be identified as author of this work has been asserted by
him in accordance with the Copyright, Designs and Patents Act 1988.

First published 2013

17 16 15 14 13
10 9 8 7 6 5 4 3 2 1

British Library Cataloguing in Publication Data
A catalogue record for this book is available from the British Library

ISBN 978 0 435 1442 03

Printed and bound in Dubai by Oriental Press

Acknowledgements
We would like to thank Bangor Central Integrated Primary School, Northern Ireland;
Bishop Henderson Church of England Primary School, Somerset; Bletchingdon Parochial
Church of England Primary School, Oxfordshire; Brookside Community Primary School,
Somerset; Bude Park Primary School, Hull; Carisbrooke Church of England Primary
School, Isle of Wight; Cheddington Combined School, Buckinghamshire; Dair House
Independent School, Buckinghamshire; Deal Parochial School, Kent; Glebe Infant School,
Goucestershire; Henley Green Primary School, Coventry; Lovelace Primary School,
Surrey; Our Lady of Peace Junior School, Slough; Tackley Church of England Primary
School, Oxfordshire; and Twyford Church of England School, Buckinghamshire for their
invaluable help in the development and trialling of the Bug Club resources.

Every effort has been made to contact copyright holders of material reproduced in this
book. Any omissions will be rectified in subsequent printings if notice is given to the
publishers.

Slimed!

Characters

Joe	the quick-thinking, imaginative and resourceful older brother of Ling and Su May
Scarlet	a spirited trainee wizard from another world
Ling	Joe's lively but stubborn little sister and Su May's twin
Su May	Joe's excitable little sister and Ling's twin
Dad	practical and serious but thinks of himself as a man of action
Mum	positive, brave and caring

Ling: Uugh! I don't like spinach!

Dad: Just eat your dinner, Ling.

Ling: No! I'm not eating spinach.

Su May: I haven't got any spinach.

Mum: No one has ... we're not having spinach tonight.

Ling points.

Ling: What's that then?

Su May: Yeuch! There's green slimy stuff on Ling's plate!

Joe: Hah! It's snot!

Mum: Joe!

Ling: Look! Some more just landed!

Dad: What on earth ... ?

Su May: Pyoo!

Joe: It smells like sweaty socks!

Mum: It's dripping from the ceiling.

Dad: That's your bedroom up there, Joe. What have you been doing?

Joe: Me? Nothing, Dad.

Su May: Oh! More! Look!

Ling: A huge pile!

Mum: It's moving!

Joe: What's that funny noise?

Dad: Yes ... that crunching sound.

Su May: It's horrible.

Ling: Like a giant munching bones for breakfast.

Mum: It's the slime! It's biting great chunks out of the table!

Dad: Get back, everyone!

Mum: I don't believe it ... the slime's gobbled up the whole table!

Joe: Look! Now the slime is disappearing, too!

Dad: What's going on?

Scarlet enters.

Ling:	Mum, Dad, behind you! It's a girl!
Su May:	She's got a cloak!
Ling:	And a little stick like a magic wand.
Mum:	What on earth ... ?
Dad:	Who are you?
Scarlet:	My name's Scarlet.

Ling:	Are you Joe's girlfriend?
Su May:	Joe hasn't got a girlfriend.
Joe:	Shut up, you two.
Mum:	Where did you spring from?
Scarlet:	From my own world.
Mum:	Your own world?
Joe:	What does that mean?
Scarlet:	Don't think that yours is the only world. There are lots. I come from mine.
Dad:	Oh, really? So how did you manage to get here, eh? Magic?
Scarlet:	Of course by magic. How else?
Joe:	Is that true?
Scarlet:	Certainly it's true. I'm a wizard. Well, a trainee wizard.
Ling:	That stick **is** a magic wand!
Scarlet:	Yes.
Su May:	Brilliant!

Mum: Why are you here? It's something to do with the slime, isn't it?

Scarlet: Yes. You see, I took away a box from an evil wizard named Shade. The box makes a very nasty slime that eats everything it touches.

Joe: It ate our table.

Su May: And our dinner!

Scarlet: Sorry. I was trying to make the box vanish when I sent it to your world by mistake.

Dad: So that's what made the slime! But ... where is it?

Scarlet: It's underneath the floorboards upstairs.

Dad: Ah!

Scarlet: I need to get it back. I only hope I can stay here long enough to find it. I'm not sure my transportation spell was good enough. I'm still learning magic and ...

Scarlet vanishes.

Mum:	Oh! She vanished!
Joe:	Her spell **wasn't** good enough.
Su May:	Will Scarlet come back, Dad?
Dad:	I don't know, Ling. But I can't hang around to find out. I'm going upstairs to find that box.

Dad goes upstairs.

Ling:	We're coming too!

Su May and Ling follow him.

Mum:	Su May! Ling! Wait!

Joe and Mum go upstairs too.

Su May:	Look, Mum! Dad's making a hole in Joe's floor.
Mum:	Be careful with that chisel, love!
Dad:	I will be. There we are ... ah! I see it!
Joe:	Is it the box, Dad?
Dad:	Yes. Got it. Look!
Su May:	Wow.

Ling:	Wow!
Mum:	Be careful with that thing!
Dad:	Don't worry.
Joe:	Look out, Dad!
Dad:	What? Aarrrgh!
Mum:	Aarrrgh!
Ling:	Aarrrgh!
Su May:	The slime came out!
Ling:	It's on Dad!
Dad:	It's crawling all over me!
Mum:	Don't touch it!
Ling:	It'll eat you up!
Joe:	Get in the shower, Dad! It might wash off!

All go into bathroom.
Dad gets into shower fully clothed.

Dad:	Brrrr! It's cold!
Mum:	It's no use! The slime's still there!
Ling:	It's munched a big hole in Dad's jumper!
Dad:	Help!

Scarlet enters.

Scarlet:	Stand aside, everyone!

Scarlet aims her wand.

Joe:	Scarlet!
Ling:	You've come back! Brilliant!
Su May:	Wow! Look at the sparks from her wand!
Joe:	Yes! The slime's gone! Are you okay, Dad?
Dad:	Phew, yes! Soaking wet, but okay.
Ling & Su May:	Hooray!
Mum:	You've done it, Scarlet! Let me give you a hug!
Ling:	Me too!
Su May:	And me!

Ling:	Come on, Joe. Give Scarlet a hug!
Joe:	Er ... no, it's all right.
Dad:	Thanks, Scarlet.
Su May:	You're a brilliant wizard!
Scarlet:	Thank you. Luckily the shower slowed the slime down a bit. That helped.
Joe:	That was my idea.

13

Dad: Are you going to take the box away with you now, Scarlet?

Scarlet: I've got it safely in my pocket. If I don't take it, Shade will come here. But I'm afraid I have another problem.

Mum: What is it?

Scarlet: The spell I used to get rid of the slime was the strongest I've ever used. I've not got enough energy left to make a spell that'll take me home.

Dad: You mean you're stuck here?

Scarlet: Yes.

Joe: We've all got energy, Scarlet. Couldn't you use ours?

Scarlet: Another brilliant idea, Joe! Quickly, everyone. Hold hands. If you create enough energy, I'll get home ... and I might be able to do something else for you. Ready?

Mum: We're ready.

Scarlet: Right ... run on the spot ... now!

The family run and Scarlet vanishes with the box.

Joe:	She's gone!
Mum:	We did it!
Dad:	Well done, everybody!
Mum:	I'm going to make a nice cup of tea.

Mum exits.

Ling:	That was brilliant. I wish we could see Scarlet again.
Su May:	Me too. I bet you'd like to see her again too, wouldn't you, Joe?
Joe:	No.

Mum calls from the kitchen.

Mum:	Hey, everybody! Come to the kitchen. Scarlet **did** do something else. She magicked us a new table!
Ling:	Scarlet's brilliant.
Su May:	Yes. She's Joe's girlfriend!

Wolfed!

Characters

| Joe | the quick-thinking, imaginative and resourceful older brother of Ling and Su May |

| Scarlet | a spirited trainee wizard from another world |

| Ling | Joe's lively but stubborn little sister and Su May's twin |

| Su May | Joe's excitable little sister and Ling's twin |

| Dad | practical and serious but thinks of himself as a man of action |

| Mum | positive, brave and caring |

Ling: Do you like dogs, Dad?

Dad: They're okay, Ling.

Su May: Do **you** like them, Mum?

Mum: Why are you asking, Su May?

Ling: Because we'd love one!

Su May: We really would.

Dad: Mmm ... I'm not sure it's a good idea.

Mum: No – not just yet. Maybe when you're a bit older.

Ling: That's not fair!

Su May: No, it's not. Come on, Ling.

Joe: Hello everybody ...

Su May and Ling go upstairs as Joe enters.

Joe: Hey! What's up with you two?

Mum: They're in a huff because we said they couldn't have a dog.

Dad: I'll go upstairs and talk to them.

Dad goes upstairs.

Joe: Dogs are great.

Mum: Not you too, Joe.

Joe: All I said was ...

Mum: I know what you said. Just ... hold on, what's that noise?

Off stage, a dog howls.

Joe: Sounds like a big dog howling ... **upstairs**!

Mum: What? The girls are upstairs!

Joe: And Dad! Come on!

Mum and Joe start to go upstairs.

Mum: Oh! What's that dark shape on the landing?

Joe: It's a wolf, Mum! An enormous wolf! Look at its fangs!

Dad enters, now a wolf, with the girls on his back.

Mum: I don't believe it ... Ling and Su May are on its back!

Ling: Hurray! We've got a dog!

Su May: A really big one!

Mum: Girls! Get down from there at once!

Dad: Raaaooowl!

Dad and girls vanish.

Joe: Oh, no ... they've all vanished!

Mum: Ling! Su May!

Joe: And where's Dad? I'll bet Scarlet's got something to do with this.

Mum: Scarlet? That wizard girl from another world?

Scarlet enters.

Scarlet: Did someone mention my name?

Joe: Scarlet! You're here!

Mum: So, Joe was right! This is all your doing!

Scarlet: Well, sort of. You see, I was on my way here for a visit when Shade, the evil wizard, saw me. He fired a transforming spell at me.

Mum: What's that got to do with us?

Scarlet: The spell missed. It travelled with me to this world and hit someone else.

Mum: Who?

Joe: It was Dad, wasn't it, Scarlet?

Scarlet: Yes.

Mum: You mean ...?

Joe: Yes, Mum. Dad's the wolf. But it's sort of good news.

Mum: What do you mean?

Joe: Well, it means that Ling and Su May are with Dad.

Mum: Oh, dear. I suppose so. But where are they exactly?

Scarlet: They're in my world.

Joe: Can you take us there, Scarlet?

Mum: Yes, we have to get them back!

Scarlet: Very well. Give me your hands, both of you. Good. Now, close your eyes.

Mum: Ohh ... what a strange feeling.

Joe: Shivery!

They travel to Scarlet's world.

Scarlet: Open your eyes.

Joe: Wow! Is this your world, Scarlet?

Scarlet: Yes.

Joe: The colours are brighter ...

Mum: And look at the size of the trees in that forest!

Joe: Listen, Mum! I can hear something.

Off stage, a dog howls.

Dad: Haaooowwrr!

Joe: It's Dad!

Su May and Ling are heard, off stage.

Ling: This is fun!

Su May: Good dog!

Mum: And Su May and Ling!

Scarlet: They're in the forest! Come on!

Joe: It's dark under the trees.

Scarlet: Watch out. You might trip over a root!

Dad, Ling and Su May are heard, off stage.

Dad: Waaaarr!

Su May: Faster, dog!

Ling: Yes, faster!

Mum: Over there!

Mum runs deeper into the forest.

Joe: Wait! There's someone behind that tree up ahead!

Scarlet: It's Shade! Watch out, he's fired a spell!

Joe: He missed you!

Mum: Raaaawr!

Joe: Oh no! He hit Mum! He's turned her into a wolf too!

Scarlet: Run, both of you! I'll hold him back with a spell ... ahh – missed him!

Joe grabs Mum's fur.

Joe: Come on, Mum!

Mum: Raowr!

Scarlet: I'm right behind you!

Joe: This way, quick!

Scarlet trips.

27

Scarlet: Oh, no!

Joe: Scarlet! What's wrong?

Scarlet: I've dropped my wand. I can't find it!

Joe: And here comes Shade!

Scarlet: Oh, where is it?

Joe: Find it quick, Scarlet! He's pointing his wand at you!

Scarlet: I can't find it!

Joe: I've got an idea! Wolf – I mean **Mum**, do you see the stick that man's holding?

Mum: Grrr ... raarf!

Joe: Great, then ... fetch!

Mum: Wuff ... rrrowl!

Joe: Brilliant! She's got his wand!

Scarlet: But Shade's after her! Run, Joe's Mum!

Dad enters with Ling and Su May.
Dad runs towards Shade.

Dad: WRAAAAR!

Joe: It's Dad!

Ling & Su May: Wheeeee!

Joe: With Ling and Su May! They're chasing Shade away! And Mum's after him too! Hooray!

Scarlet: Thank goodness! And look, I've found my wand!

Joe: Here come Ling and Su May with Mum and Dad.

Ling: Look, Joe: we've got two big dogs now!

Su May: Two! Brilliant!

Joe: Er ... well, not quite ...

Scarlet: Ling, Su May, come over here. That's it, now ... watch.

Su May: Why are you pointing your wand at the big dogs, Scarlet?

Ling:	Yes, why? Oh, look at the sparks!
Su May:	The big dogs have changed ...
Ling:	... into Mum and Dad!
Dad:	Hello, everyone.
Mum:	Thanks, Scarlet. It's good to be back.
Scarlet:	Not at all. Thank Joe, too. If he hadn't had the idea for you to fetch Shade's wand, then we all might have four legs and fur by now.
Joe:	It was nothing.

Ling:	But now there aren't any dogs!
Su May:	Not even one!
Mum:	You know what, girls? I feel differently about dogs now.
Dad:	I do too. So, how would it be if, once we get home …
Mum:	We all go down to the dogs' home and get a puppy?
Ling & Su May:	YEEESSSS!!